Beaver Steals Fire

Beaver Steals Fire

A Salish Coyote Story

Confederated Salish and Kootenai Tribes

Illustrated by **Sam Sandoval**

UNIVERSITY OF NEBRASKA PRESS   LINCOLN AND LONDON

This project is made possible through the generous support of the following:

U. S. Department of the Interior, Bureau of Indian Affairs

National Interagency Fire Center, Boise, Idaho

Montana Committee for the Humanities

Manufactured in China
⊗
Set in Skia and Adobe Garamond
and designed by R. W. Boeche
Printed by Everbest Printing Company

Library of Congress Cataloging-in-Publication Data
Beaver steals fire: a Salish Coyote story/
Confederated Salish and Kootenai Tribes; illustrated by Sam Sandoval.
p.   cm.
ISBN-13: 978-0-8032-4323-1 (hardcover: alk. paper)
ISBN-10: 0-8032-4323-5 (hardcover: alk. paper)
1. Salish Indians—Folklore. 2. Kootenai Indians—Folklore.
3. Coyote (Legendary character)—Legends.
I. Sandoval, Sam, ill.
II. Confederated Salish and Kootenai Tribes.
E99.S2B43 2005
398.24 5297725'089979435—dc22
2005006484

To our elders and ancestors
who shaped and maintained our cultural landscape with fire.

To our contemporary fire warriors
who courageously face fire and are putting fire back on the land.

To our children yet to come who will inherit this cultural landscape.

Germaine White

ACKNOWLEDGMENTS

The Confederated Salish and Kootenai Tribal Division of Fire enthusiastically supported the proposal to develop culturally relevant fire education material, of which this book is one piece. That support remained throughout the duration of the project.

We thank Tony Harwood, Dennis Dupuis, and all those regional and national fire managers who recognize this project as a model for other tribes. Thanks to David Rockwell for his contributions to this project.

This story represents thousands of years of oral tradition. We have tried to remain faithful to our elders in our interpretation. In *Beaver Steals Fire*, fire is a gift from the Creator brought by the animal beings for human beings who are yet to come. Fire remains an important gift in our traditional ways of knowing and understanding.

G.W.

A NOTE TO THE READER

We must ask one special favor of those who use this book in the classroom or who may otherwise read or discuss it aloud: our traditional Coyote stories—the legends of Coyote—and the other animal people that appear throughout this book—should be told or discussed only during winter when snow is on the ground. The elders usually bring out the stories in November and put them away again when the snow is gone—usually by late February or March. Some say the stories are put away when the snakes come out. It is said that snakes will come to those who do not follow this custom or that cold weather will come during the warm months. Coyote stories, like other parts of our traditional way of life, are part of a seasonal cycle. By following this tradition readers, teachers, and students can enjoy this aspect of our culture— keeping and saving something for the time of year during which it belongs.

Salish and Pend d'Oreille Culture Committee

A long, long time ago, the only animals who had fire lived in the land above, up in the sky. The animals on earth had no fire. They gathered and had a meeting. They wondered how they could obtain the fire from the sky world. The animals were very cold and needed to keep warm during winter. They made their decision, and they said, "The one who has the best song will be the leader of the raiding party to the sky world to steal fire."

Ččlexʷ (Muskrat) was the first to sing, but his song was no good.

Then the other animals sang their songs. Still they were not satisfied.

They heard someone whistling from a little hill a short distance away. Quickly they went there and saw Snc̓le (Coyote) and his friend Ćsqáńeʔ (Wren). Wren had many little arrows.

They told Coyote, "You must come to our meeting lodge."

So Coyote went to the meeting lodge, where he was asked to sing. Coyote sang his song. Immediately they liked his song, and they began to dance.

That was when Coyote was appointed leader of the raiding party.

Coyote met with the raiding party. He told them, "Not far from here is the opening that leads to the land above. That is where we will enter."

The animals asked, "How are we going to get up to the opening to the sky world?"

Wren said, "I'll shoot arrows one above the other to make a ladder into the sky."

When Wren finished shooting his arrows into the sky, he was the first to climb up because he was the lightest. He carried with him a little rope made of bark. He climbed until he reached the land above, and then he lowered the end of his little rope.

The animals began to climb the rope. Smҳe ('Grizzly Bear') climbed last. Because he was such a greedy person, he carried his lunch with him. He had two large bags of food. Grizzly Bear climbed halfway up the rope, and it broke. His bags were too heavy. Grizzly Bear fell tumbling back to earth.

In the sky world, Walwi (Curlew) was the guardian of fire.

Coyote gathered the members of his raiding party together and said to them, "I want to find Curlew's camp."

Coyote said, "Curlew is down at the river right now. He's watching his fish traps." Coyote said to Łmłama (Frog) and Sxʷnu (Bull Snake), "Follow Curlew back to his camp. When you find his camp, come back here and let us know where it is."

Frog and Bull Snake went to the river. They saw Curlew sitting on the bank watching over his fish traps. Soon Curlew stood up and headed for his camp. Frog and Bull Snake followed. They reached a little hill, and over this hill was the camp. Frog and Bull Snake crawled up to the top of the hill. Very carefully they peeked over and watched Curlew go into his lodge.

Bull Snake began to get hungry. He licked Frog's foot. Frog said, "Quit." Bull Snake soon swallowed the foot, and Frog said, "Quit." Frog's other foot was swallowed. Frog said, "Quit." Frog was swallowed up to his waist, and he said, "Quit." Bull Snake swallowed one arm, and Frog said, "Quit." Frog was swallowed up to his neck and said, "Quit." Then Frog was gulped up, still saying "Quit." You could hardly hear Frog. Then there was silence.

When Bull Snake returned to his companions, Coyote asked, "Where is Frog?"

Bull Snake said, "He was eaten up." He didn't tell Coyote who ate Frog. Bull Snake continued, saying, "But I found Curlew's camp. He has the fire there."

Coyote said, "Sqlew̓ (Beaver), you will be the one who steals fire."

Beaver said, "OK. I'll go to the river. I'll pretend I'm dead and float on my back on top of the water. Curlew will think I'm dead, and he will catch me and bring me back to his camp."

Coyote said, "Pqĺqey (Eagle), when Beaver is at Curlew's lodge, you fly there and land in the top of Curlew's lodgepoles and pretend that you are wounded and unable to fly. When Curlew comes out and sees you wounded, he will ask his family to come outside and capture you. They will leave Beaver alone just long enough for him to steal fire."

Eagle said, "OK. I understand."

Beaver went to the river and floated downstream, pretending he was dead. Curlew was guarding his fish weir and saw Beaver floating on the water. He took his fish weir and caught Beaver. He said, "I'll take Beaver back to my lodge for his soft fur."

Curlew's family asked, "What are you going to do with Beaver?"

Curlew said, "I'm going to skin him and dry his hide. I have use for Beaver's fur."

It wasn't very long before Curlew and his family heard noise outside. Something had landed on top of their lodge.

Curlew went outside and saw Eagle. Eagle
pretended he was wounded and couldn't fly.
Curlew thought, "I'll kill him for his feathers."
He called for his family.

Curlew told his family, "Kill that eagle. I want him."

They began to climb up the lodge to get Eagle.
Just as they were about to grab him, he flew away.

Meanwhile, Beaver was alone inside the lodge.
That's when he stole fire.

Then he sneaked out of Curlew's lodge.

Once out of the lodge, he ran to the river. Curlew saw him and cried out, "Beaver came back to life and stole fire!" They chased him.

But Beaver jumped into the water.

Curlew told Tupń (Spider), "Go downstream and spread out your web to capture Beaver."

Spider went downstream to set his web, but Beaver had gone past, holding the fire. Three times Spider went downstream to set his trap, but Beaver had already passed.

Beaver arrived at the place where all the animals had climbed up the rope. He climbed down. Coyote and the other animals of the raiding party followed.

Curlew wasn't too far behind. He looked down and saw that the animals were already passing the fire back and forth to each other and carrying it back to their camp.

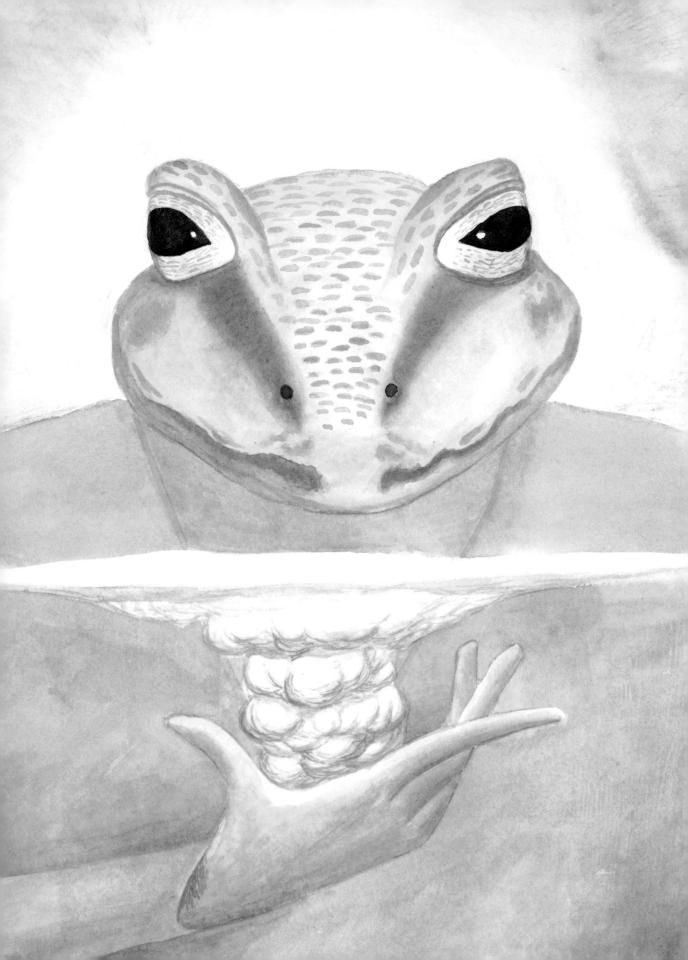

Curlew, who had his own frog in the sky world, called his frog and said to him, "Make it rain so the fire will go out."

Curlew's frog made it rain. It rained for a month, but the fire didn't go out.

Sq̓ʷo (Prairie Chicken) was the last person the animals had given fire to. When Curlew's frog made it rain, she sat on the fire, and it kept burning.

That is how the animals brought fire to us.

The End

A Note to Teachers and Parents

According to the traditional beliefs of the Salish, the Creator put animal beings on the earth before humans. But the world was cold and dark because there was no fire on earth. The animal beings knew that one day human beings would arrive, and they wanted to make the world a better place for them, so they set off on a great quest to steal fire from the sky world and bring it to the earth. That is the story told in this book, a story that reminds us that while fire can be a destructive force, it is also a gift from the Creator brought to us by the animals.

In our tradition—that of the Salish and Pend d'Oreille of the Northern Rockies—fire is a gift that can nurture life and be used to take care of the earth we have been entrusted with. It provides us with light and warmth. It makes it possible for us to cook our food. It is at the heart of our spiritual practice and at the very center of our traditional way of life. Before European-Americans arrived, it was the tool that our people used to intensively manage the lands where they lived. Our ancestors burned areas to increase food and medicinal plants. They burned to improve forage for game animals, like deer, elk, bighorn sheep, buffalo, antelope, and bear. They used fire to hunt by building drivelines and game surrounds, and they used it in warfare, both offensively and defensively. They burned prairies and meadows to keep encroaching trees and brush at bay, so their horses would have plenty of grass. They groomed trails and cleaned their camps with fire. For thousands of years our ancestors more than doubled the frequency of natural fires. Indeed, the plant and animal communities we have inherited today are in large measure the legacy of Indian burning. Those communities have adapted to fire, and many species are fire dependent. This early landscape was not a virgin landscape in the sense of being untouched by humans but a cultural landscape shaped by thousands of years of tribal use of fire.

Salish tribal elder and historian John Peter Paul talked about the tribal person whose role it was to set fires. This man was called Sxʷpaám, meaning literally "Makes Fire" or "Fire Setter." He possessed an intimate knowledge of fire and its effects on plants and animals that he acquired from his own experiences and inherited from generations of Sxʷpaám before him. He knew that the diversity of plant species doubled after burning, and that if done properly, both wildlife and people would benefit from periodic fires. For example, he knew that the productivity of huckleberries increased dramatically about twenty-five years after a fire. Huckleberries were a staple not only of Indian people but also of grizzly bears, black bears, and dozens of birds and small mammals; all of them prospered from the periodic burning of huckleberry fields.

One need only compare middle to late nineteenth-century photographs of the mountains in northwestern Montana with the way those mountains looked at the end of the twentieth century to see the profound influence that fire, both natural and Indian lit, had on this landscape. The introduction of European diseases in the late 1700s, which diminished Indian communities, and later, the growing presence of European-Americans themselves, gradually put a stop to traditional Indian burning practices in the Northern Rockies. By the late nineteenth century, Indian people who attempted to practice traditional burning encountered violent hostility and government repression from many non-Indian communities. Non-Indians also extinguished lightning-caused fires whenever they could. Since then those fire-dependent landscapes have changed dramatically.

Place names in our language tell us much about the historic relationship between our tribe and the land. Indeed, place names are of great importance to our people, because they often record information about the cultural ecology—how the land was used and managed. In some cases, place names tell us where fire was used in beneficial ways to maximize plant and animal resources. But the place names—the oldest parts of our language, which often come from Coyote stories and describe the making of our homeland or its resources—no longer have meaning because the places have changed so much in the absence of fire. Big Prairie in the South Fork of the Flathead, once an important camping area for Salish people, is an example. What was a series of expansive clearings kept open by frequent burning is now just a little prairie, and the surrounding, once park-like stands of ancient ponderosa pine are now dense with Douglas-fir trees.

Today, because we have excluded fires, we face many problems in our forests—the risk of catastrophic fire as well as very dangerous conditions in what land managers call the wildland-urban interface, the place where human settlements meet the forest. Many of these problems have their roots in our society's failure to appreciate the depth and sophistication of the tribal relationship with the land and in particular tribal land management practices.

It takes a long time to create and maintain large old pine forests and open prairies. The landscape that was known and managed by the Salish and Pend d'Oreille people is now a vanished landscape. As a society, we are trying to recover that older tribal landscape that took twelve thousand years of habitation, experience, and occupation to create.

The most basic question our society is faced with now, as we attempt to return fire to the land that Indian people formerly burned, is How do we do it? How do we restore that lost cultural landscape? The traditional tribal view of fire can enrich and inform the technical view of fire management. The traditional view draws from deep unseen roots—like the story told in this book—but it can nevertheless inform each new generation that learns to value it. The traditional tribal use of fire, and perhaps more important, the tribal view of fire, can provide guidance as we try to repair a landscape that science tells us is now at risk.

This story teaches our children how difficult it was to bring fire from the sky world and how important it was to animals and humans. Now it is time for humans to return the gift of fire to the animals.

The Artist

Sam Sandoval creates his artwork on the Flathead Indian Reservation in western Montana. He attended the Institute of American Indian Art and has created art as far back as he can remember. Sam currently works as a media specialist for the Salish and Kootenai Tribal Preservation Department, which is dedicated to the perpetuation of tribal cultural resources. He hopes one day to apply his artistic endeavors toward moviemaking. Sam lives with his wife, son, and daughter near Dixon, Montana. This is his first book.

The Storyteller

Johnny Arlee was raised by his grandparents with Salish as his first language. He has worked tirelessly throughout his life to pass on the traditional culture and way of life of the Salish and Pend d'Oreille people. In the 1970s and 1980s, Johnny played a key role in developing the Salish–Pend d'Oreille Culture Committee into a nationally respected tribal cultural institution. Johnny is the author of three books: *Coyote Stories of the Montana Salish Indians*, *Mali Npnaqs: The Story of a Mean Little Old Lady*, and *Over a Century of Moving to the Drum: The Salish Powwow Tradition on the Flathead Indian Reservation*. He has served as technical advisor, actor, and scripting consultant on several feature-length motion pictures, including the classic *Jeremiah Johnson*. Presently Johnny serves as cultural advisor for the Salish and Kootenai Tribal Health Department. He lives in Arlee, Montana.

The Fire History Project

This book is one part of a larger fire-education project. The project includes an integrated set of educational materials focusing on the use of fire by Indian people and the profound effects that Indian burning had on plant and animal communities. The materials also discuss fundamental principals of fire ecology in the Northern Rockies, the changes that have occurred in vegetation as a result of fire exclusion, and how and why fire is being restored to the landscape.

The project materials include:

- this storybook for children, based on the Salish tale *Beaver Steals Fire*

- a video based on the storybook

- an interactive DVD for middle school and older students on the traditional use of fire told through elder interviews, a photo gallery, a database on fire-dependent species, historical information, and perspectives from fire managers

- lesson plans on the history of fire use, fire ecology, and fire management, and

- a Web site for anyone seeking information about the Indian use of fire and the Salish and Kootenai Tribes' forest management plan, which relies heavily on prescribed fire to accomplish its restoration goals.

A Brief Guide to Written Salish and the International Phonetic Alphabet

by Shirley Trahan,
Salish-Pend d'Oreille Culture Committee Language Specialist

Introduction

The written Salish that appears in this book uses a form of the International Phonetic Alphabet (IPA), a writing system developed by linguistic anthropologists to represent all languages in the world. The form of IPA that we use has been refined for the Salish language through many years of careful work by tribal elders, Salish–Pend d'Oreille Culture Committee staff members, and linguists.

Most sounds in Salish are also found in the English language and can be represented with English letters. A number of Salish sounds, however, are not found in English and cannot be represented using the English alphabet. Here is the complete Salish alphabet:

$$\text{Λa} \quad \text{Cc} \quad \text{Ċċ} \quad \text{Čč} \quad \text{Č̓č̓} \quad \text{Ee} \quad \text{Hh} \quad \text{Ii} \quad \text{Kk} \quad \text{K}^{\text{w}}\text{k}^{\text{w}} \quad \text{K̓}^{\text{w}}\text{k̓}^{\text{w}}$$

$$\text{Ll} \quad \text{L̓l̓} \quad \text{Łł} \quad \text{Mm} \quad \text{M̓m̓} \quad \text{Nn} \quad \text{N̓n̓} \quad \text{Oo} \quad \text{Pp} \quad \text{P̓p̓} \quad \text{Qq}$$

$$\text{Q̓q̓} \quad \text{Q}^{\text{w}}\text{q}^{\text{w}} \quad \text{Q̓}^{\text{w}}\text{q̓}^{\text{w}} \quad \text{Ss} \quad \text{Šš} \quad \text{Tt} \quad \text{T̓t̓} \quad \text{Uu} \quad \text{Ww} \quad \text{W̓w̓}$$

$$\text{X̣x̣} \quad \text{X}^{\text{w}}\text{x}^{\text{w}} \quad \text{X̣}^{\text{w}}\text{x̣}^{\text{w}} \quad \text{Yy} \quad \text{Y̓y̓} \quad \text{ƛ̓ƛ̓} \quad \text{ʔ}$$

As you may notice, Salish contains both unglottalized and glottalized versions of many sounds or letters. Glottalized sounds are pronounced "harder" or "longer" than unglottalized sounds. For instance, the Salish *p* is much the same as the English *p* in the word *people*. The glottalized Salish *p̓* sound is like the regular or unglottalized *p*, but is made with an extra push of air—a slight pop. Similarly, the glottalized *m̓* is pronounced with more emphasis than a regular or unglottalized *m*. These differences may sound subtle to an English speaker, but they make for complete differences in meaning in Salish words. For example, the Salish word *pin̓*, which has a regular *p*, means "bent." But *p̓in̓*, with a glottalized *p̓*, is the root for the verb *to crowd*. For this reason it is crucial that glottalizations and other phonetic aspects of the language be represented accurately in our written system.

Sounds in the Salish Language

The Vowels

 a the vowel sound in the English words *far, car,* and *are*.

 e the vowel sound in the English words *end, yes,* and *wed*. If there is an *e* at the end of a word, it is pronounced. In Salish, every letter is always pronounced; there are no silent *e*'s in any of the words.

 i the vowel sound in the English words *see* and *week*.

 o a sound in between the vowel sounds in the English words *road* and *bought*.

 u the vowel sound in the English words *cool, moo*, and *boo*.

The Stops

 c a sound similar to the English *ts* sound at the end of the words *cats* and *rats*.

 č the soft *ch* sound in the English word *church*.

 k the *k* sound in the English word *key*.

 k^w the *k* sound pronounced with the mouth rounded. It is similar to the start of the English word *quick* but is made slightly further forward in the mouth.

p a sound like the English *p* in *paper* and *people*.

q a sound similar to a *k* but pronounced farther
back in the mouth or throat.

qʷ the *q* sound pronounced with the mouth rounded. It is similar
to the start of the English word *queen* but is made slightly farther back in the mouth or throat.

t the *t* sound in the English words *to*, *hot*, and *at*.

The Glottalized Stops

c̓ the *c* (*ts*) sound pronounced with glottalization (harder).

č̓ the *č* (*ch*) sound pronounced with glottalization.

k̓ʷ the *k*ʷ sound pronounced with glottalization.

ƛ̓ a clicking type of sound that combines the *t* and *l* sounds.
It is called a lambda.

p̓ the *p* sound pronounced with glottalization, producing a
slight pop.

q̓ the *q* pronounced with glottalization.

q̓ʷ the *q̓* pronounced with the mouth rounded.

t̓ the *t* pronounced with glottalization, producing a slight pop.

The Fricatives

s the *s* sound in the English words *say* and *yes*.

š the *sh* sound in the English words *shut*, *push*, and *wish*.

h the *h* sound in the English word *hot*.

ł   the sound made by pushing air along the sides of the mouth with the tongue behind the teeth. It is called a barred L or unvoiced L.

x̣   a friction-like sound produced in the same area of the mouth as the *q*. (To learn this sound, begin by producing a sound much like softly clearing the throat.)

x̣ʷ   an x̣ sound made with the mouth rounded.

xʷ   a sound similar to the *wh* sound in the English word *whoosh* made with the mouth rounded.

The Resonants

l   a sound similar to the English *l*.

m   a sound like the English *m*.

n   a sound like the English *n*.

w   a sound like the English *w*.

y   a sound like the English y in the words *yes*, *pay*, and *yarn*.

The Glottalized Resonants

ĺ   the *l* sound pronounced with glottalization.

m̓   the *m* sound pronounced with glottalization.

n̓   the *n* sound pronounced with glottalization.

ẃ   the *w* sound pronounced with glottalization.

ỷ   the *y* sound pronounced with glottalization.

The Glottal Stop

ʔ   a sound made by simply closing and opening the vocal cords. It abruptly cuts off or starts a sound and is used before or after a vowel in some words. A glottal stop is similar to the break in the middle of the English expression "uh-uh" indicating "no."

Long Vowels and Long Consonants

In words with double consonants, each consonant is pronounced separately.

In words with double vowels, each vowel is pronounced separately. This pronunciation makes the vowel sound longer.